I0743075

S F
BOOKS

SPARK & FIZZ BOOKS PRESENTS

PLANET SCUMM

AUTUMN 2019   "A WRINKLE IN SLIME"   ISSUE NO. 7

— A FAITHFUL TABLE OF CONTENTS —

EDITOR IN CHIEF	CREATIVE DIRECTOR	MANAGING EDITOR	EDITOR	MARKETING
SEAN CLANCY	ALYSSA ALARCÓN SANTO	TYLER BERD	ERIC LOUCKS	SAM RHEAUME

COVER BY ERIKA SCHNATZ | ERIKASCHNATZ.COM   SPOT ART BY ALYSSA ALARCÓN SANTO | ALYSSASANTODESIGN.COM

Planet Scumm is a triannual short fiction anthology. Visit **planetscumm.space** for submissions.

© SPARK & FIZZ BOOKS

First Printing, 2019   ISBN: 978-1-970154-03-0   Portland | Boston | New York

MISSION: SCUMM

... And we're back. Folks, your pal Scummy's been catching a lot of stories on the old "Slime-wire" about some kind of rough-and-tumble intergalactic mercenary hired by the Earthers. Word is this killer's hunting down whoever was responsible for destroying the Earther planet. You may remember that joint from one of my previous broadcasts—Planet Scumm landed on Earth not too long ago, and had one plasma-hot rager of a party. This would have been... oh, just before the Earthers claim their planet was destroyed. Good thing Scummy skedaddled when he did, eh?

Anyhoo, pity the poor galactic denizen in this merc's crosshairs. Now, the latest reports from across the galaxy.

Speaking of ragers, culture correspondent **Donald Jacob Uitvlugt** comes to us this week with a run-down of the latest in alternative genocide. It's called "Dance Dance Apocalypse," and it's sweeping across imperial hegemonies small and large. For some, dance isn't just a way of life, it's a way of saving a life— or millions.

If the jumpin' and jivin' nightlives of the colonized don't interest you,

Frank Smith's latest might. In "The Nearest Far-Away Place," we get a wrenching-yet-hopeful tale of one aging spacer's quest for love—or something like love—among the stars. This one moved even a cold soul like mine, folks, and I don't have a particularly strong grasp on this so-called "mortality."

Planning a vacation to your nearest phantom planet or quarantine zone? You're certainly not alone, this time of year. But whether it's a hike through an abandoned pathogen lab or a picnic on a mass grave, it's important to remember that apocalypse preserves are delicate former ecosystems, easily disturbed by the introduction of self-replicating lifeforms. Nature correspondent *Rebecca Gransden* gives us just such a cautionary tale in "Zone 59."

From the politics desk is *Aaron Emmel's* latest, an exclusive peek at the inner workings of a conquered planet. In "The Perpetual Empire," Emmel follows a resident of the North American Subjugate, in a society that views compassion as the ultimate sign of weakness. Scummy doesn't think you're weak if you love, baby, but he just loves to make you weak, if you know what I mean! I'm talking *compromised immune system*, my pretties.

Noah Lemelson's "At the Border Post" gives us a first hand account of that age-old profession: guard duty. Guarding what? Guarding who? Who knows—*that's* who! The bosses aren't telling and we don't want to know. Though now that I mention it, your pal Scummy has had a guard or two on him back in the day. Yep, I was in the slammer. The hoosegow. The big hard-to-escape box place. And even though we were on opposite sides of the whole detention question, I respected the hell out of those guards. Not enough to, like, *not* kill them, but still. *Respect*.

Finally, let's have a little chat about *Hailey Piper* and her most recent report, "Reptile." Time anomalies might be a common occurrence for the well-to-do in the galactic core, but on some backwater plan- ah.

Oh, uh, sorry folks. I've got more to say about this crackerjack story, but it appears some sort of—what would you call this—*intergalactic mercenary* has burst into my recording studio. Blaster drawn, no less! I'm going to sign-off for now, so remember: *If it isn't undulating in panic and trying to remember just who Scummy pissed off recently, it isn't... Planet Scumm!*

[END TRANSMISSION]

A WRINKLE IN SLIME

Spark & Fizz Books 2019
Portland | Boston | New York

AUTHORS

DONALD JACOB UITVLUGT lives on neither coast of the United States, but mostly in a haunted memory palace of his own design. His short fiction has appeared in numerous print and online venues, including *Cirsova Magazine*, Flame Tree Press's *Murder Mayhem* anthology, and *Planet Scumm* issue 2. Donald strives to write what he calls "haiku fiction," stories that are small in scale but big in impact. If you enjoyed "Dance, Dance Apocalypse," let him know via Twitter: @haikufictiondju.

FRANK SMITH is a writer based in Austin, Texas. His stories have appeared in *Analog Science Fiction and Fact*, *Asimov's Science Fiction*, and *The Awl* (RIP). He has an MFA in creative writing from The New School and is a member of the SFWA. Frank spends most of his time chasing after tiny humans. Visit him at frank-smith.com.

REBECCA GRANSDEN lives on an island somewhere along the coast of the United Kingdom. A fervent advocate of the DIY ethos, she tries to read and support as many indie and self-published writers as she can. She has been published at Nightmare Press, *Soft Cartel*, *X-R-A-Y*, Burning House Press, and The Cabinet of Heed, among others. Her books are *Anemogram*, *Rusticles*, and *Sea of Glass*. Some of her stories will be featured in the soon-to-be-released collection, *Cardboard Wall Empire: Volume One*.

AARON EMMEL and his stories have appeared in numerous magazines and anthologies. Thanks to the patience of his wonderful wife, and despite the impatience of his wonderful children, Aaron also writes essays, graphic novels, and interactive fiction. Find him online at aaronemmel.com.

NOAH LEMELSON is a young speculative fiction writer based in Los Angeles. He received his MFA in Creative Writing at the California Institute of the Arts, where he studied under the mentorship of Brian Evenson. Noah has previously published short fiction in online magazines such as *Space Squid*, *Allegory*, and *Silver Blade*. You can find more of his work at Noahlemelson.com

HAILEY PIPER grew up in a patch of creepy northeastern American woods where ghouls and monsters filled her imagination. Today she draws on those childhood nightmares as an editor of official documents and as a writer of primarily horror who can't shake her love for sci-fi and fantasy. Her short fiction has appeared in esteemed publications such as *Blood Bath Literary Zine* and *Black Rainbow, Volume 1*, and she's a proud two-time *Planet Scumm* contributor (previously issue 6). Her debut novella, "The Haunting of Natalie Glasgow," can be found on Amazon.

DONALD JACOB UITVLUGT

DANCE DANCE APOCALYPSE

Tonight would be the last time.

Mitsuko looked at the clothes laid out on the bed. In the past, her outfits had been her armor. But no amount of armor could protect her against the cold, bitter fact of last night's deaths. She couldn't go on doing this. After tonight, she would tell the General she quit.

Yet she owed it to her fans, to the faithful who still believed in her in spite of the evidence, to go out in style. With a slow sigh, she dressed. She pulled on pink fishnet stockings and then a white skirt with a hundred pleats that ended just above the knee. Her white tube top sparkled with sequins. The sleeveless white jacket reached to the floor, lapels and hem trimmed with pink faux fur. She slipped into hot pink platform shoes, repeating a mantra to herself as she wound the straps around her ankles.

Last time, last time, last time.

She studied her reflection in the mirror and adjusted her spiky wig. Then she stenciled a star in glittering body paint under her left eyelid. *There.* She was ready to save the world. *One last time.*

Mitsuko hurried out of her apartment, down to the lobby, and out past the gauntlet of fans. She closed her eyes against the flash of camera phones. *I hope I don't look as tired as I feel.* She was sick of the whole thing. She made a blind dash for the back seat of the awaiting car.

She sighed and sank into the leather seat. The door blocked out the rest of the world, at least for a few moments.

"They love their hero."

Mitsuko's eyes snapped open at the driver's bitter sarcasm.

"I'm no hero. I'm just a dancer." *And after tonight, not even that.*

The driver nosed them into the city's stop-and-go traffic. Even with the fate of the world in the balance, life went on. People worked hard to pretend things were normal, mindlessly buying and selling to distract from the sword hanging over their heads. "You're right. You're not a hero. You're a collaborator. Helping the damned aliens keep the rest of us in line."

The car slowed. Mitsuko held her breath and forced herself to look out the tinted car windows. The helicopters confirmed her fears.

"That's right. A new crater. Don't worry. We'll still make it to the club in plenty of time."

They inched past the destruction. It was as if a giant had taken a bite out of the city. Buildings sheared in half, pipes and wires that just... stopped. In the center, a black pit yawned greedily.

"My sister..." The driver's voice cracked. "My sister and her kids. They used to live on that block."

Mitsuko's stomach flipped. If the driver hit the accelerator right now, they would sail over the barriers into the crater. Game over.

Do it. I'm sick of the bullshit too.

Instead, the driver turned away from the destruction, toward the club. Mitsuko exhaled slowly.

"I'm sorry about your loss..." She checked his nametag in the mirror. "Thomas."

          DANCE DANCE APOCALYPSE

"I don't give a fuck about your 'Sorry.'"

Anger flared insider her. "If that's how you feel, why'd you even show up for work today?"

Thomas laughed bitterly. "I have a job to do, don't I?"

"Well, so do I."

Mitsuko stepped out of the car before it had completely stopped. She hadn't asked for this responsibility. Like everyone after the conquest, she'd gone through the aliens' testing not knowing what they were testing for. When she was chosen, her first thought was that the Otaku were going to eat her.

A man in a black suit and dark glasses waited for her in the alley behind Invisible Face Cream Arena. He opened the back door to the club and she stepped inside.

Music. The heartbeat of a world dancing for its life. She took a moment to fix her makeup. She didn't cry. Not Mitsuko. Anger and fear flowed through her system, moving with the beat. Part of her wished Thomas had had the guts to do... something.

This is it. Tonight's my last dance.

She handed off her purse to another suit and stepped from the hallway into the club itself. Rainbow lights strobed and reflected off the dancers. Mitsuko saw flashes of spiked hair, writhing snake tentacles, glowing fiber optic strands. Dancers wore skin colored chrome, vermilion, chartreuse, indigo. Textures whirled past her: silk, fish scales, stainless steel.

General Shining Aspirin Radar approached. Mitsuko forced a smile as she greeted the supreme commander for the Otaku of this sector. Today he had formed his body into the shape of a nineteenth-century maharaja, complete with turban, sash, and military decorations.

He pressed his palms together and bowed to Mitsuko.

"Your opponent awaits, o champion of Earth."

"All right. I'm as ready as I'll ever be."

Shining Aspirin Radar scowled at Mitsuko's lack of formality. *Screw him.* Tonight was her last night. She would act however the hell she wanted.

The General turned and led her through the dancing throng of aliens dressed as humans and humans dressed as aliens. The dancers writhed together, the music penetrating them all. Music, the universal language. Music had drawn the Otaku to the planet Earth. Decades of music, beamed without thought into the depths of space. The Otaku had followed the transmissions back to their source.

Now music was the only weapon against them.

"It's her. It's really her!"

The words rippled through the dancers. As recognition reached critical mass, a shout rose up, drowning out the music.

"MIT-SU-KO.

MIT-SU-KO.

MIT-SU-KO!"

Otaku and human alike chanted her name. She did her best to hide her confusion. Why would the enemy cheer her like one of their own? It didn't make sense. Then again, little about the Otaku made sense. That was the Otaku. Apes of humanity, masters of Earth.

A space opened up in the midst of the dancers as the General led her forward. White tile gleamed back the powerful spotlight. Mitsuko's opponent stepped out toward them.

His skin was the color of a starless night. She couldn't make out features, not even his eyes. The place where his lips should have been he had rouged the color of fresh blood. He sported a colony of blood-red pseudopods instead of hair; the tendrils undulated in time with the beat, like someone had fashioned a wig from the guts of a dozen lava lamps. His

outfit was all zippers and red leather.

Mitsuko nodded to her opponent. "Good dancing, Euphonious Blue Jeans." She had never danced against him before, but he had a reputation as a tough opponent. Her last dance ought to be a good one.

The Otaku gave no sign he had heard her. General Shining Aspirin Radar held up his arms. The immediate silence hurt the ear. Light turned his outfit electric white, with sparks of diamond, ruby, and sapphire.

"Ladies and gentlemen, Otaku and humans." The crowd held its breath. "Let's dance!"

🖫

The crowd cheers and the music erupts again. Mitsuko's muscles tense. The ceiling of the club shimmers into a display of the skies above the city, complete with the hundreds of rainbow-hued Otaku satellites. Lasers shoot from half a dozen points. In her peripheral vision, Mitsuko sees Euphonious Blue Jeans start to move. *And tonight's battle is on.*

Mitsuko sweeps her arms in front of her and pumps out her fists. The laser beams hit the shields she conjures and diffuse into iridescent fireworks.

The crowd roars and joins the dance They leave a respectful circle around the combatants.

          DANCE DANCE APOCALYPSE

A series of running-man steps. The satellites spit out mines, a net of destruction enveloping the city. Mitsuko sways her hips. Her shields detonate the mines, all but a couple that impact in the suburbs. The viewscreen shows the explosions. Water erupts from a swimming pool, dirt flies off a front lawn. A rhythmic flash reduces a quaint two-story to rubble.

Too easy. This isn't like Euphonious Blue Jeans' reputation at all. There. Mitsuko spots the slow seekers while they are still within range of her shields. *Step, step, shoulder, shoulder, shimmy.* The viewscreen lights up in pyrotechnics. Another cheer. Mitsuko curses as she sees one of the seekers slip through. The club building shakes and Euphonious Blue Jeans' death toll points roll up. More cheers.

The moves come in faster combinations. Mitsuko can no longer keep Euphonious Blue Jeans in her peripheral vision. She focuses on the screen. *Clap, spin, clap, spin.* A little John Travolta disco for flare. Sirens sound. Combination points rack up for Mitsuko as Euphonious Blue Jeans' death rays and missiles explode into harmless glitter and rainbows.

She can feel anger radiating off Euphonious Blue Jeans. The Otaku don't like to lose.

The beat picks up, and Mitsuko hears Euphonious Blue Jeans move in an elaborate series of clog steps while his arms whirl about him. But she has found her groove now. Her platforms slap against the floor, keeping perfect time with Euphonious Blue Jeans. The point counters spin. Bombs and missiles explode as soon as they launch. Lasers criss-cross the sky.

The rhythm drives her. She is the music. The club lights sizzle against her skin. Sweat steams off her body, incense for this sacred rite. She is grace. She is motion. She is all that is good and noble in the human race.

The club trembles. A cheer rises as another Otaku missile makes it through. She thinks of Thomas' sister and curses herself for getting too cocky. Euphonious Blue Jeans is almost a blur beside her. The screen fills with glamorous death.

No. She is Mitsuko, champion of Earth. The best damned dancer on the planet. She shake shake shakes off her doubts and fears. Her groove is back and she steps, bops and rocks to it. As fast as Euphonious Blue Jeans is, she is faster. It's now a question of endurance.

The cheers, screams and applause of the crowd become part of the music. The beat penetrates all, pounding in an orgy of sound. Mitsuko reaches over her head, as if she could snatch down the death machines and crush them by will alone.

Her shields deflect a missile into one of the Otaku satellites. She has never seen that happen. Right before the device flies apart, the screen grows dark. The music cuts off. Euphonious Blue Jeans is on his knees, panting. Mitsuko is victorious.

Utter silence. Then the club erupts in applause.

"Ladies and gentlemen, Otaku and humans. I give you your winner: Mitsuko!"

After the applause, the music started up again. The empty space around Mitsuko collapsed. Human and Otaku danced, celebrating loss and victory with equal vigor.

General Shining Aspirin Radar swooped in before the dancers crushed her. He led her to a corner of the room. Mitsuko had no idea what happened to Euphonious Blue Jeans.

"Excellent. An excellent score, a new record for your species. I must congratulate you yet again on being your planet's ablest champion."

His praise rang false. She had hurt them, Mitsuko realized. A possible future flashed in her imagination. One where the Otaku's own weapons were turned against them. Mitsuko and the other dancers around the world, perhaps on a single given day, would destroy the belt of satellites ringing the planet and free the human race.

As quickly as the image flashed into her mind, she knew it would never work. *There's too many of them. They're too strong.* If the human race truly hurt the Otaku, the fun and games would end. *They'd just stop the dances and wipe us out.*

"Look at them celebrating your victory."

She couldn't tell the difference between human and Otaku as they swayed, gyrated and thrashed. They would have danced the same if Euphonious Blue Jeans had beaten her. The Otaku had already won the war.

"Why don't you join them, Mitsuko?"

It would be so easy. Tired as she was, she could just let the music carry her away. Give up, like she had planned. Go out on top. Even the Otaku loved Mitsuko, the Champion of Earth.

She paused at the thought. The dance united both species. As long as they kept dancing, humanity went on. The human race danced on the edge of the abyss, and tomorrow they might fall over into oblivion. *But we didn't today.*

Mitsuko smiled back at General

      DANCE DANCE APOCALYPSE

Shining Aspirin Radar. "I don't think I will tonight. I have to rest up for tomorrow, after all."

The General nodded, dismissing her. The car was waiting for her at the back door. Thomas said nothing to her as they drove through the city streets. People were already out surveying the damage.

Televisions in shop windows showed footage from tonight's dance. Passersby cheered as she won. Some of them danced along with her, right there on the sidewalk.

"She was your biggest fan." Mitsuko could hardly hear the driver's voice. "Little Nora wanted to be a dancer too, when she... when she grew up...."

She considered resting a hand on the man's shoulder, and then thought better of it. Instead, she tried to put as much compassion into her voice as she could. "We can't change what happened. But we can go on living. For them. Every day we're still fighting is another victory."

Thomas said nothing. Mitsuko sank back into her seat. Her body ached for bed, but in her mind she was already planning tomorrow's outfit. Something green, perhaps. She liked green. She hummed as she choreographed moves in her head. Tomorrow she would dance the battle for Earth all over again. She would be ready. *She would win.*

FRANK SMITH

THE NEAREST FAR-AWAY PLACE

On the space stations, the mining colonies, the inns for wayward travelers built into asteroids, the generation ships where many live in-between lives, and on the habitable moons that are our new homes, we carry our boxes of photographs of the people we have met so we can remember who we are.

We are careful not to touch the paper's grain and bleed an image away. Like the gravitons stored below the decks of our starships, my wooden box of photographs keeps me from floating away. The hinges of the box creak, the corners are dented and chipped, and the cherry finish is rubbed away from the lid. Instead of storing holos on my reckoner, my photos are printed on a variety of materials: heavy stock, cheap paper (green and fading), and dull metal plates.

In the photographs, I see Rowan, my red-haired love; Azariah, the commander of my first star ship; Landry, the homeless child I should have helped; and the bartender on Helios Creed.

Whenever I pass a mirror, I am reminded that I spent my most vital years in the depths of space. Hard travel and strange environments have taken their toll. I am gray. My eyes are bad. My bones are brittle. Walking is difficult. From pelvis to head, my body feels like a thing not meant to stand upright, but instead to be dragged behind me as I limp forward.

In my photos, I remain that young person—wavy black hair, full hips, and bright green eyes. I am still me.

Today, I live on a mossy rock surrounded by an artificial atmosphere. The rain hammers down on this moon. The oxygen is clean. The breeze carries the scent of flowers in the fields, food being cooked in the other cottages on my isle. Life. Nature. Existence.

I am fortunate, yet most days I can't stand it.

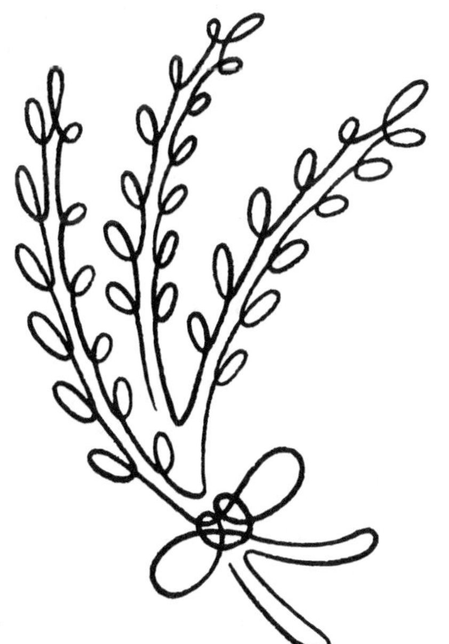

The air on the mining ship where I ended my career was spicy, like halitosis, like compost. On the shuttle that took me down to this moon, the oxygen was so strong with lavender that it tasted like the purple stuff parents give their babies when they have fevers.

Perhaps only recycled star-ship oxygen smells good to me.

I miss it all. I miss the sensation of being in transit. The vibration of distant engines under my feet, the rumble of the oxygen recyclers, the purposefully dull glow of the LED lights.

My Rowan would laugh at sentimental old me. I can still remember the soft and heavy sensation of my love's heart beating so close to my cheek. Strong hands on my back. A husky voice breathing my name.

In the photograph, Rowan is frowning, uncertain. Our love was terminal. I did not qualify for the same generation ship as Rowan's family. I'd waited too long to apply. I'd have to wait for the next one. Our great-great grandchildren might meet up again on a habitable world picked out for us in Tau Ceti—but we would not go there together.

Things could have been different had we been married. We were young and marriage was such a commitment. We weren't sure if we wanted to live and die together onboard a ship that would carry our babies and their babies through interstellar space.

In the photo, printed on the best stock available on my homeworld, my love's forlorn brown eyes are filled with care, full lips pulled into a tight smile. We'd just argued and it was time to part. No wrinkles beside my love's eyes. No gray hair. How can I be so old that an eighteen-year-old looks like a newborn baby to me? I stand beside Rowan, and I look... Is it relief washing over me? Yes. I was young enough to think I'd still find someone better out there.

Instead of taking a place on the next generation ship, I signed onto a merchant starship. My plan was to travel before making any kind of commitment. That was the easier solution to the real problem, I thought. On the trader's ship, we zipped from one colony to the next, bartering for what each planet had to offer.

On my home world, Ornth, one day equals twenty-four hours. The closest world to trade with us is Ara Martis, where each day is twenty-five hours long. On the outer rim's planets and moons, a day can be as few as ten hours long. On starships, it is nighttime all the time. We pretend to keep track of the days, with the computer scheduling our calendars. And yet, when we come across other travelers, the calendars are always off by a few days, weeks, and months. No matter how short the day, the lonely night will always come sooner than you expect, and it's hard to call a planet your home when you're always a year or two away from seeing it again. The starship becomes home.

Azariah, the commander of my ship was an ill-tempered, raggedy, sour person prone to dark, drunken moods. Azariah always wore the same blue jumpsuit with stains all over its front, worn-out boots, long hair too stringy to pull back in a ponytail. In the photograph, printed on a thin metal plate, I can tell my commander knows my plans to leave. That weathered face with its penetrating gray eyes was staring through me, angry for the work that would be lost—that I'd cost him.

We traveled to colonist moons where we traded vegetable oils and grains from Ornth that could be converted

   THE NEAREST FAR-AWAY PLACE

into biofuels and plastics. We carried livestock, weather satellites, antibiotics, and anything else that might have value.

In between moons, we often stopped at a space station orbiting the planet Sath, seventh from our local star.

I knew and trusted a garment maker who owned a boutique on the Sath station. The garment maker, Kel, sold simple fashions and provided tailoring and repairs. I've always spent my every available credit on new fashions, and I take care of my things. We were good friends.

Kel let me hide in the storeroom until my starship had left. Kel told me later that Azariah had been in a rage, tearing up and down the marketplace searching for me.

"I can't imagine what it was like to work on that ship," Kel said.

"Yes, you can."

During my years with the trader, I saved up enough money to return to Ornth and yet I never could find the time to book the trip. My parents were long gone by then, but I could have started over—joined another generation ship, figured it out along the way. Instead, I remained on the station, mending garments, running the cleaning machines, doing whatever task was available.

Working with the textiles I had shipped in from the colonies, I created my own designs. Nothing extravagant. I made functional clothing—rain-resistant coats, slender-cut trousers, cotton sweaters, inner layers that could keep you warm when you caught a chill or wick away the sweat when you felt stuffy. Each item was created with meaning. I wanted the wearer to feel that they were dressed in their favorite thing. I designed the patterns for each piece of fabric, made each detail intentional.

To those in the know, my styles were in high demand. And though I never turned much of a profit, I kept the business running after Kel passed away.

Kel never allowed me to take a picture, saying: "Keep me in your memory."

I can still see Kel, stooped over a clattering sewing machine, programming the printer to create a new pattern, or standing in front of the store watching the travelers pass through the space station's bazaar. Kel put back a bottle of Galilean whiskey a day, and could hold it like no one I'd ever met. Kel was sallow and puffy toward the end, nearly bald with only wisps of silver hair, hands turned into claws by arthritis The booze is probably what did it. But, then again, all of us that choose to live in space live shorter lives.

Kel taught me to be kind. That's how I met the child living in the unused corridors of the space station. The child coexisted with the other runaways and those left-behinds. Because I bought or traded clothing and apparel from the traders that made their way through the station, I always had more than I needed. So I donated second-hand bundles of clothing to the station's homeless whenever I could.

Kel kept an eye on the lost and left-behind—making sure they had clothes, credits, food. I was just going through the motions, giving away clothes that didn't sell to make space in the shop. I felt an obligation, and little more.

The child wore shoes that had no soles, torn pants that stopped mid-calf, a ragged T-shirt, and a cloak made from an old blanket. The child's name was Landry. While on a vessel heading to the outer rim colonies, Landry's parents had died from malnutrition. The ship's captain abandoned Landry on the station.

I offered the child clothes, taking care in my choices so Landry would have clothes that fit and spare things for the days ahead. Good clothes. Useful things.

Landry insisted on paying me back, offering to work in the shop. Instead of doing what Kel had done for me, I asked for a photograph. I don't know why. Kel would never have asked for anything in return. In the faded photograph printed on cheap paper, I can see a small dirty face staring back at me with resentment, a bundle of clothes clutched against the child's chest. As soon as I had the photo, Landry was gone, hurrying away to the darkest part of the corridor. I saw Landry a few time after that, and the child never seemed well—undernourished, filthy, a ghost. I imagine Landry died alone in some darkened corner of the station.

How privileged of me. How selfish. If not for the garment maker's pity, I would have been trapped on Azariah's ship forever.

It took me a long time before I understood that a few spare clothes wouldn't have saved Landry, nor would a job. I've never been lost, never been without work or the ability to get work. And it is always that way for many of us. A job would have done the child good, helped Landry find a way. But a job is just a job. Landry needed someone's attention. Their care and affection. Their time.

And then, one day, Azariah returned. Having fallen on hard times, the captain wanted to square up on old debts. There I was, running my little shop with its modest profits. No threat to anyone, except Azariah claimed I'd cost the ship money, work, and time—and this required compensation.

Azariah had arrived with an order from a local magistrate. The magistrate

THE NEAREST FAR-AWAY PLACE

ruled that I was in the wrong. As such, I was required by law to turn over all of my assets—including the shop—for the outstanding time owed on my contract.

The quiet times ended. I fought the order and appealed to the higher courts. I offered to pay out Azariah for my contract, set up a stipend until the debt was paid. I tried everything I could to keep the shop. Meanwhile, the magistrate hit me with violation after violation, until I could no longer afford to stay in business.

I shuttered the store. Liquidated my assets. Paid off Azariah in full. I walked away broke.

Too old to start over with a new business, I signed on with the only starship that would take me—a mining hauler, exploring the asteroid belt for new claims.

And yet. I could have returned to Ornth. I could have found a way forward.

The mining ship was a hard-used bucket of bolts that the crew spent more time patching up than flying. Entire sections of the ship operated without gravity, including the engineering rooms where I ran our configurators and repaired the mining equipment. We harvested platinum, cobalt, and water from local asteroids.

I committed to the work and kept at it, losing track of the time. Those were the years when I stopped taking photographs. Try as I might, I can't remember anyone's name from this time. All I can see is Landry. There's a good chance I helped send more than a few Landrys into the asteroid mines.

During a stopover on Helios Creed, I decided I'd had enough. Helios Creed is a small space station—an inn for miners and traders—built into an asteroid at the edge of the belt. I'd learned not to sign work contracts, and yet, my boss was surprised when I quit, like the company had been doing me a favor asking me to destroy my body for them.

"You'll never work for a mining company again," said my boss.

"That's fine," I said. I was all used up anyway.

Free from all commitments, I plunked down on Helios Creed for a few weeks, while waiting on the next passenger ship to Galilea to come along. I had saved up enough credits that I hoped to buy a little place on Galilea, a terraformed moon surrounded by an atmospheric dome, and live out the rest of my life.

Because I ate at the same tavern, sat on the same barstool every meal, I became friends with the bartender at the local pub. The bartender was also from Ornth. Brown eyes like my red-haired love, a hint melancholic from the years spent tending bar in a nowhere place, same grayish skin as me from years in space. My last night we got to talking about our regrets, which is what seems to happen when you're in a strange bar in a strange place. I laid it all out, from leaving Ornth, to Azariah's ship, to my little shop, to the mining company, all of it but the most important part of my story—the reason why.

And the bartender, patting a head shaved clean said, "I have my regrets, too. I should have stayed on that generation ship. They don't like you to leave. But the ships make stops, picking up more passengers on the way out of the system. Without knowing I was leaving the ship, I left. Stayed behind when we stopped at a space station circling Sath. Told no one—not even my family. Once you leave, you can't go back. Life goes in all its different directions, but the ships keep moving along the same orbital path—with or without you."

"Why'd you do it?" I said.

"I had someone once," the bartender said. "I thought I could find them again. When we were young, we dreamed of the new worlds our babies and their babies would explore. But, it's a big galaxy and life moves fast. I've been here since I stopped looking."

And in that moment, all the years living in transit became clear to me. "May I have your picture?" I said.

"No one has asked me for a picture in years. Why would you want a picture?" The bartender leaned back, arms crossed. Closed off to me. Wary. Uncertain.

Placing the photograph of Rowan, my love, down on the scratched and pitted surface of the bar, I saw us as we were and how we'd been in all the years between, and I said, "Because I remember your red hair."

REBECCA GRANSDEN

ZONE 59

Only three days in. Hooded, ready to be transported to a location it was better for me not to know. There would be no time to acclimatise. They would need to capitalize on my defection, most likely still undetected.

A small, stocky man named Horace pulled on the rim of thick black material and fastened the hood. He stepped up close, clammy and wheezing, fiddling with the ties to ensure I couldn't shake the hood off, not that I would've tried. Only days ago I'd been at my desk, imagining what being a terrorist would be like. Now I had a taste.

Horace took my arm and led me forward, through a long, echoey corridor and then outside. The dry heat of the afternoon made me gasp. Machinery whirred in the distance. Footsteps approached across the dry, gritty surface. I felt Horace move away from me and stomp back the way we'd come from.

"I'll take you from here," said a measured voice, with only a slight quaver. This new guy bundled me into a transport. The machine groaned—an obsolete, older model—and we set off to god-knows-where.

I stepped out of our ride and into the tepid night air.

"Wait a sec," Arch said. I heard the low *whoosh* of opening a compartment at the back of the transport.

"Can I take this off yet?" I said, impatient to get out of the hood. Tantalizing wisps of cool air swept past me.

"Oh sorry," he said, distracted, "knock yourself out."

I fumbled with the wide knot at the base of the hood and lifted the material away from my sweat-soaked head.

I stood for a moment, as blurry lights floated before me in the dark. I rubbed my eyes and cleared the sweat from my vision as best I could.

Dark sand reached ahead and carried on in shadow until it hit a strange barrier. Almost translucent, the wall pulsated with a low white light. Inside I could see the glowing outlines of tiny desert creatures, lit up like photo negatives. The majority seemed to be insects, some in flight making light trails, some crawling along the base of the barrier, all in a slow procession. They avoided colliding indicating they had an awareness of each other. A larger creature approached, a desert fox, shining brilliantly, and stalked the length of the barrier, passing through the mass of glowing insect bodies, oblivious to me.

"Don't go near it," Arch said, heaving a metal box out of the rear of the transport. "It will suck the life out of you. No mercy."

I turned to him and all I could manage was a blank expression.

Arch lowered the metal container to the ground and began dragging it forward, edging it closer to the barrier. "That wall, my friend, is one of a kind. I think the folks who had been working on Project Grey needed something to set their minds to after the shit hit the fan. A way for them to redeem themselves, I guess, though publicly they took no responsibility, of course."

Spectral fireflies danced along their designated path behind Arch as he struggled with the box.

"You're not telling me that this is Zone 59, are you?"

"I'm not telling you anything. You'll see for yourself soon enough."

Zone 59. The secrecy made sense, then. A quick memory grab and anyone could discover it. I looked at Arch and regretted ever agreeing to switch sides. Up until now, this group - the group I'd been a part of for just a few days - had committed only minor disruptive acts, mostly against virtual infrastructure.

That's what I'd signed up for. Not *this*, whatever this was.

"Why me?" I said.

"Because you are not flagged. You are a nonentity, no one is looking for you—yet. I've worked for years to erase my trail, just for a night like this. That's why we've been chosen. I can't guarantee that no one will get hurt, but that's not our intention. We've figured this thing out. We know how to target it so that the whole network will be compromised. You've seen what we do and why we do it. This is the next level, that's all. Now help me with this."

Arch stopped a few meters short of the barrier and opened the box. I approached, just as he raised a creature from inside it. Grabbed by the neck, it squirmed in his grip. It appeared to be some kind of modified armadillo.

"She's been trained to walk toward the light, which is poetic, considering what's about to happen to her."

"I don't like the sound of this."

"Look, it's not pleasant, but one sacrifice is all we need to end the tyranny of interfacing, of jacking, of memory acquisition, all of it. The wall feeds on life itself. Anything that touches it instantly drops dead and everything that is 'life'—all those electrical signals, that pulse of blood and information, or the soul if you so desire—becomes part of it. Those insects are the most recent of the countless others that have flown into the wall, blissfully unaware of what that means. Once the life is sucked out of them, a kind of echo remains—pure energy. Eventually the glow fades, only to be replaced by the next swarm flying over the desert." The creature started to wiggle. "Lucy here will be a legend. She's unique, you see. The energy that keeps her alive is the key."

"Her life force."

"Yes. When she touches the wall, we'll have a short window to pass through the barrier. There are buckets in the box." I reached in and took one. "When I let her go, follow her slowly. Wait for my okay before approaching the wall. Are we clear?"

"Don't worry, you can go first."

Arch nodded. He crouched down and turned Lucy toward the parading lights of the wall ahead. He let go of her and picked up his bucket, his eyes remaining on the creature as she sniffed the night air. After a moment's pause, Lucy scuttled forward.

I held my breath as we neared the wall. Close up, the illuminated insects were mesmerizing. I held back a little as Lucy became a moving shadow, transfixed by the wall's glow. Lucy exhaled one last time, and her small frame tipped to one side. An armadillo's silhouette appeared in the wall, and joined the parade of shining insects. Arch beckoned me forward and held up a palm for me to stop when I'd stepped close enough. "Give it time," he said, a concerned look on his face.

'How will we know?" I whispered.

The wall dimmed, and the color faded into a deep purple.

'"That's it. We're in." Arch bounded straight through the barrier, which was a good two meters thick. He waved at me from the other side as purple flies danced between us. "Come on. We've got maybe twenty minutes."

I strode up to the barrier and stepped through, eyes closed

I opened them to a vast panorama, waves of undulating dunes in dark metal gleaming under moonlight, like a dead, frozen ocean. Every now and then the purple lights around the perimeter reflected across the deactivated nanobot grains.

I remember seeing interviews with the survivors—the scientists who made it to the roof of the research station before it was consumed. They wept as they recounted how they had left their colleagues behind, about how they didn't have time to think. The nanobots evolved so quickly, replicating and consuming at a rate they hadn't anticipated. The research station must be out there somewhere, underneath all this. Or maybe there's nothing left at all. No one knows how the wave was stopped, though most suspect a sophisticated EMP.

I stepped forward, transitioning from desert sand to the crunch of deceased nanobots underfoot.

"Fill it up, man," Arch said, his bucket already full and waiting at his feet.

I scooped as many nanobots as I could into my bucket and fastened the lid. "These things are dense," I said. I could barely lift my haul.

We traveled along a dirt track toward the rising sun. Eventually we arrived at a large boulder and the transport juddered to a stop. Arch disembarked and walked over to a crag, brushed away the sand by his feet, and lifted a metal access door.

We struggled inside with the buckets, down some metal steps and along a barren corridor. Arch took us into one of the far rooms where Horace was waiting.

Horace rose from his stool and patted Arch on the back. I got a nod, which was acknowledgment enough for a new guy, I suppose. The room was small and mostly dark apart from the center, where a transparent chamber, similar to an incubator, sat on a table.

Horace led Arch to the table and motioned for his bucket. I placed mine on the concrete floor, as it was now clear that I held the backup

Horace sighed dreamily, "Thank you, men.". He opened Arch's bucket and picked out a single nanobot with some tweezers. Carefully, he placed it into a small compartment inside the chamber. A robotic arm retrieved the nanobot and dropped it onto a raised cushion.

"All being well, we should only need one," Horace said, smirking, 'I never thought this day possible."

"Tell the kid," Arch said, nodding his head in my direction. "He deserves to know what he's been part of today."

"Alright," Horace lowered his face as close as he could to the chamber and gazed at the lonesome nanobot. The light hit him strangely, and made his eyes appear black.

"Years of research has led us here. We can finally infiltrate the network directly, with these." His eyes scanned the tiny dot longingly. "They can access anything - biological, technological, or any combination of the two - and influence their host from inside. It will be possible, for example, to program one of these little lovelies to enter the body of a politician and compel them to change their vote. This has been planned for years. That's why you are to stay here— for as many years, if need be. Now that you know what the purpose of all this is, we can't allow you to leave I'm sure you were aware of what you signed up for."

I nodded. I didn't think I had been fully informed, but it appeared that was irrelevant now.

Arch sensed my apprehension. "We are vanguards, man. We're only beginning to grasp the potential of what we can achieve now that we've discovered a way to reactivate these machines in a controllable manner."

"The tech behind the wall is similar. The same scientists worked on it. We followed their principles to find a way to utilize the nanobots. It was a long shot, but it actually worked!"

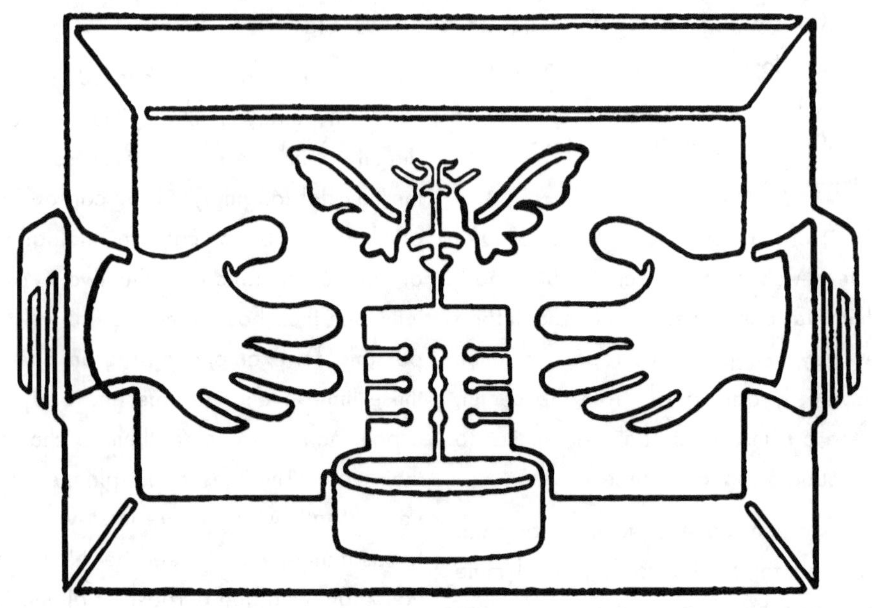

Horace placed his hands into protective gloves on the side of the quarantine chamber. I moved closer to watch. In one corner of the chamber sat a small plastic container potted with tiny holes. Horace clicked open a clasp on the top of it and a miniature door opened. A beetle scuttled out, its wing cases reflecting the harsh artificial light with red and green iridescence.

"It knows to go to the middle for its food," Horace said. He extracted his hands and flicked a switch. The inside filled with a smoky, white plasma, thin enough to see through. "Same conditions as the wall," he said, as though I should be impressed. "We have replicated the same process of harnessing energy as it filters through biological organisms. This is the trick: We modify the transfer in a more sophisticated way than they were able to even dream of. I can't believe they didn't make the connection." The beetle was confused by the plasma, its antennae twitching and searching. "Come on, Dwayne," Horace said, "Your time has arrived."

The bug ran straight for the tray at the center of the chamber. Quicker than my eyes could follow, the insect was on the nanobot. It instantly keeled over, the nanobot stuck to its right foreleg.

Horace froze.

A second passed, and then the nanobot rose and hovered a few centimetres above Dwayne's corpse.

Horace laughed and sat back down on his stool, shaking his head and rubbing his face.

"Congratulations," Arch went to shake Horace's hand. Before he could grab it he turned back toward the corridor. "Do you hear something?"

Horace raised his head and cocked an ear. "I hope not.".

"Oh god." Arch took off down the corridor.

Horace went pale, but stayed where he was. "But we disengaged the hive mind," he said, muttering, "But we thought of every eventuality."

I ran after Arch and out into the blaring desert sun. Arch was by the transport, hand shielding his eyes, looking out along the road we'd traveled to get here. From my position, I saw it. High dark wisps, like a swarm of insects off on the horizon, over Zone 59.

"This can't happen, this can't happen." Arch staggered backwards, then turned and sprinted for the door by the boulder. "Get inside!"

I backed towards the entrance but thought better of it and headed for the transport. Inside, I instructed the vehicle to run at full capacity in the opposite direction. A fearsome roar grew louder, behind me. I hurriedly reconnected the communication dashboard to the worldwide network and sent a message: "Zone 59 active. Help. Repeat. Zone 59 active."

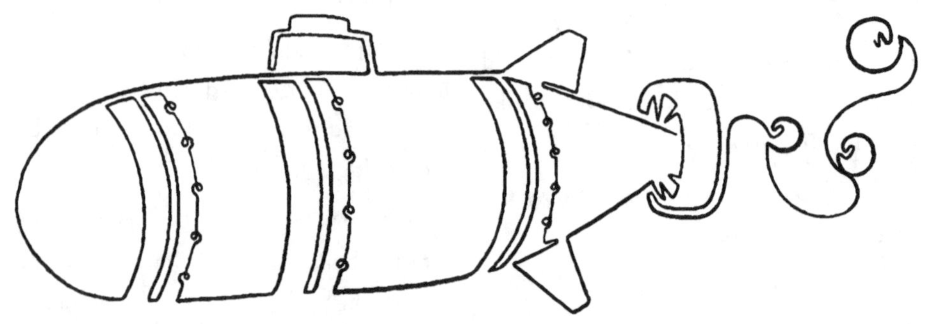

AARON EMMEL

THE PERPETUAL EMPIRE

The walls sweat condensation and radiate cold. I try to keep to the center of my cell, but it's hard not to move, and moving almost always means brushing up against one of the sides. My thin uniform absorbs the water and clings to my skin.

It's always damp, and I'm always cold.

The walls are glass, and so are the ceiling and floor, and beyond them in every direction is darkness, the black weight of water pressing down from above and surrounding me.

Sometimes, illuminated by the dim light-tube above me, I see a shadowy shape twist by outside. Once I saw a tail or a fin strike the glass with a slap. I can't see far enough through the murky water to know what the creatures are. I never know when they'll return.

From my prison, I have three connections to the outside world. First: the thin hoses that snake down to deliver an oxygen and nitrogen mix to the chamber, and remove carbon dioxide. When I'm falling asleep, I'm terrified that one of the swimming creatures will rip them loose. When I wake up, I pray that one of them will.

Second: twice a week a small submersible comes to deliver boxes of chalky, tasteless food pellets and bottles of fortified water. Sometimes the submarine brings three or four old comic books from disconnected genres and series. I think they send me the books to keep me from going crazy. At first, I thought it was because they wanted me alert enough to suffer from my isolation. Now, I have another theory: I think they're keeping me here to interrogate me. The Empire is worried about my economic projections, and doesn't want to risk anyone else hearing what I know.

The airlock used by the submarine is the only portal large enough for a human to fit through, but it's been impervious to all my attempts at escape. The only other opening is the transparent system of tubes that vents my waste into the surrounding water.

My third link to the outside world the water itself. Somehow one of the worst tortures of this place is not knowing where I am. It's possible I'm at the bottom of an ocean or lake. I imagine the lake is artificial, and sealed in a vast bunker, or in a satellite orbiting Earth or one of the New Cities. Other times, I dream the lake is underground.

But now the submarine is returning. I can hear its hum before I see it. Someday, there will be people on it. Otherwise, I insist to myself for the thousandth time, why wouldn't they have already killed me? This place is a prison, but isn't it too elaborate to be only a prison?

If there are people on board, I won't tell them anything unless they first tell me where I am.

I have always been waiting for the Empire's agents to come for me, and even here, locked below water, I am waiting for them now.

🖫

Air dreadnaughts filled the sky above me. I was on my way to meet the imperator of the North American Subjugate at the Cleveland garrison to present him with a proprietary report of Citadel Reinsurance's underwriting projections for the next fiscal year. I was going to warn him of famine.

I had memorized all the data, but I still had no idea what I was going to say. Would he want to know what was coming, so he could prepare, or would he want me to lie, so he could deny knowledge and blame my superiors when the worst came? The right answer would bring me one step closer to becoming a quaestor. The wrong one could cost me my career and freedom.

That's what I was absorbed with when the woman in front of me dropped her crate of apples on the street. She was probably thirty, but walked like someone far older. Judging by her cheek tattoo and the pain knobs jutting from her neck, she was a refugee from one of the coasts, now indentured to an Ohio farm.

I froze. Just for an instant. But then I recovered and kept walking. I hoped it would look like I had only stumbled. No one would notice.

That's what I told myself.

Down the block was a World Walker whom everyone else was avoiding. Across the street a group of vocational students, middle schoolers, were having an energetic competition to see who could recite the longest list of statutory punishments. No prescribed mutilation seemed beyond their scholarship.

Then one of the kids saw the woman. "An infiltrator is wasting the empire's food!" he shouted. He laughed and started toward her. Theft was a capital offense. But if they destroyed the food she had "thrown away," it wasn't theft.

The woman dropped to her knees and scrambled to collect the apples that had rolled away.

I walked past the woman and the kids.

"Does your boss know you throw his produce away?"

"Did you come here to destroy our food, infiltrator?"

From the students' voices and footsteps, I could hear them spreading out behind me. I hesitated again, for a longer moment. This time, it clearly wasn't a stumble.

The World Walker turned toward me and stared. Her body—genetically engineered to be stronger and faster than mine could ever be—seemed taut with restrained force. She leaned forward, ready to unleash it.

Keep walking, I told myself. I was so close. If I impressed the imperator, if I became a quaestor... my parents would despise me, but they were already disappointed in me for striving so openly to serve the Empire. That's what I assumed, anyway; they were of course afraid to tell me what they truly thought. But if I became a quaestor, I would be able to travel throughout the subjugate, perhaps one day anywhere on Earth or even off it, and I could access pre-Imperial texts, and someday—but it was too dangerous to finish that thought. Everyone has tells. Your subconscious mind can betray you.

One of the students behind me had grabbed the woman's pain knobs. That was the only thing that could have produced such a sudden, sustained

 THE PERPETUAL EMPIRE

shriek. I heard someone else kick her crate away.

I forced myself to start walking again. I recited the first of the Empire's Evident Truths to myself: *The weak infect the strong. The strong protect themselves by destroying the weak. That is how the Empire grows in might.*

The screaming stopped. I heard the crate snap and splinter. I heard heels pound the fallen apples into the asphalt. Then the teenagers walked past me, laughing and congratulating each other. It was all a performance. Maybe they had enjoyed attacking the woman, but that's not why they did it so loudly. They did it so people could witness them enjoying it.

To betray the strong is to betray the Empire.

The students and those like them, not the World Walkers, are the Empire's true enforcers. The Empire encourages distrust so that when its enemies fall, none of us will want to lift each other up.

I heard her moan behind me.

And then I sealed my fate.

This time, I didn't just stop. I turned.

Out of the corner of my eye, I saw the World Walker leave the sidewalk and stride toward me. Pedestrians scattered out of her way.

The woman was still on the ground, on her knees. It wasn't the pain that kept her there. It was the anger and shame. The knowledge that if she rose she would say what she wanted to say, lash out the way she wanted to lash out, and then she would be crushed just like the fruit all around her. Maybe I was just projecting. But I recognized the look in her eyes, even though I'd never permitted it in my own.

I stood in front of her.

The World Walker stopped, just a few paces from me, watching me. Waiting.

I could kick her, and prove myself.

Or I could just stare, maybe even sneer, and walk away. That would probably have been enough to save me.

But instead I knelt before her. I took a breath. Then I held out my hand.

She reached for it, but she never made it. The World Walker grabbed my arm and hauled me up. Forceflex cuffs were snapped over my wrists. I had been about to help an indentured laborer. And now, I am here.

The hum of propellers grows louder. The submarine appears as a shadow in the water, and then it's close enough that I can see its curved hull. This one is bigger than the craft that brings me food and comics. It looks strong enough to survive enormous pressures. I am not in a space station. I am not in a lake.

The submarine connects to the airlock, and its hatch opens. Two quaestors step out in crimson armor, a male and a female. I haven't seen other humans for... weeks? Months? My heart pounds so strongly I'm afraid I'll pass out. I'm ashamed of the stench about to greet them. I tense, planning my impossible escape. I don't see a way to get out alive, but I don't need to be alive.

The outer airlock door closes, and the inner door opens. Both quaestors enter the cell. I'm backed against the wall. Their faces are in mine.

"Jordan Rane," the man says.

I swallow and nod. I don't see weapons on either of them, but if I can grab him quickly enough and shove him into the woman—

"Jordan," says the woman, "you may wonder why you are here, a mile under the ice of Europa."

"You know the risks the Empire is facing, even better than its rulers do," the man says. "You know its weak points."

The woman studies me. "This is one of the few places we hold in the solar system where we can gather without fear the Empire will overhear us. Keith can stay here in your cell for the next twelve hours to convince the monitors you haven't left."

"Left? Where?"

"Our base is nearby," Keith says.

The woman smiles. "We were watching you back on Earth, Jordan." She takes my hand in her gloved fingers. "Welcome to the revolution."

My first thought isn't of politics. It's of space to run. A wide space, filled with light.

I start to shake her hand. Then I pull mine back. This is all too neat, too simple. "I'm staying here."

She blinks. "Did you hear what I said? You can help us. We can take you out of here."

"No."

"Jordan-"

"I know how the Empire works. You're not getting anything out of me."

"You can help us," she repeats.

"I'm not telling you anything."

Eventually, they go. I stand with my arms crossed in my suspended cage, watching their craft depart. I can hear its engines fade in the deep, long after it is swallowed by darkness.

NOAH LEMELSON

AT THE BORDER POST

Click. Bzzzz. Click. Bzzzz. Click. Bzzzz. Click. Bzzzz.

Virge took a puff. He flicked the ashes of his cigarette off his sweat-dampened button-up as Ted clicked through the channels, one, two, three, on the small TV that sat on the desk.

"Not much to watch," he said to the buzz and the flickering shapes of nothing.

"No signal," said Virge, "not out here."

Click. Bzzzz. Click. Bzzzz.

Virge stared out the window of their booth, itself the rough size, shape, and décor of a shipping container.

"Clouds and mist," he muttered, glancing through the soft glow of night. His cigarette smoke wandered its way up towards the ceiling, only to be devoured by the cut and groan of the fan.

"You'd think they'd make sure the TV worked," said Ted.

"Who?"

Click. Bzzzz. Click. Bzzzz.

"What else are we going to do?" asked Ted.

"Our jobs?"

"Well that ain't hard."

Click. Bzzzz.

"Posters, two," Ted said. "TV. Ceiling fan. Cigarette packs. Bucket. Gas mask. Boxes, four. Cabinet. Trash bin. Intercom panel. Bookshelf, small..."

He was walking circuits around the small room as Virge tallied the inventory on a sheet.

"...Yoga ball, deflated. Chairs, two. Microwave. Light bulbs, four."

"Don't forget the doors and windows," said Virge.

"Those can't be on the sheet."

Virge tapped the list with his pen. Unchecked boxes lay aside 'Door: front' 'Door: basement' and 'Windows: front.'

"Oh, well, they're all there too."

Virge grunted, and Ted sat down.

"So what now?" he asked.

"We wait."

The mist ocean was a midnight blue, and stretched as far as Virge could see. Sometimes the sky, a similar but tad softer monocolor, would seem to light up a moment, as if heralding dawn, though the sun never arrived.

"How often do boats come by?" Ted asked.

"Now and then."

"How can they float on that?"

Virge lit another cigarette, "How should I know? I'm not a physicist." The texture of his cigarette smoke matched the sea, and he wondered, not for the first time, if it was the same stuff, only bluer.

"Why can't the ships go around? Why do they have to stop at our gate?"

"Why do you have to ask so many questions?" Virge said.

"Because I'm new."

"Are you now."

"What?" Ted asked.

Virge shrugged and sucked in, letting the smoke massage his lungs.

"Is there a manual or something?" Ted spun around in his chair.

Virge jabbed his finger at the bookshelf.

Ted kicked the ground, skidding his chair across the linoleum.

"It's not there," he said.

"Well what is?"

Ted picked up a large green block. "A Gentleman's History of the Textile Industry: Volume 4."

"Read that."

AT THE BORDER POST

A deep tidal moan rolled out over the mist.

"You know I think I loved her," said Ted.

Virge squinted out at the horizon. Sometimes it looked like there were mountains poking up at the end of the world.

"I really did," Ted continued. "It was that smile of hers that did it. Knew a lot of girls, but no one smiled like her. Not open mouthed, not closed, but in-between. You know? Couldn't see the teeth."

If he squinted long enough, maybe he could catch the mountains moving. Just maybe.

"She was popular. Busy. A lot of men wanted to see her, but no one else ever said anything about her smile."

Ted scratched himself.

"I heard a lot of talk about her hair," he continued. "She was proud of it. Blond. You know how it is. Men go crazy over blonds."

"And you don't?" Virge said. There, it moved. Maybe.

"No. I think it must have been dyed, anyway. The point is, her smile."

💾

Virge was writing in his red notebook. Halfway through. It was a story about a boy and a goat, on a hill. He had written others like it before. The boy always starved by the end. He wasn't sure why the boy didn't eat the goat. It was right there, had its neck leashed by a rope, yet the boy never even tried. Maybe this time he would.

Ted was clunking around on the dock outside. Clunk. Clunk. Clunk. He didn't need to make so much noise. Maybe it was because he didn't have anything else to do. The dock was small, not much to explore, just a square ring. It wasn't connected to anything, except, by wires, to the tripod camera pole a dozen meters out, and of course, on all sides, the mist, which was about as nothing as anything could be.

💾

Clunk. Clunk. Clunk.

Virge wrote some more. He tried adding some poetry to his story, with the boy singing verse to the goat. Maybe that would help. He wasn't sure of the words, couldn't hear them right, but good stories had poetry in them, at least as far as Virge remembered.

The door opened with its familiar groan, Virge not looking up until Ted leaned over him.

"Surprise!" came a muffled call, as Ted tossed out a bucket. Gassy blue fell upon Virge, like a sandslide of ice. Virge scrambled off his chair, blinking and coughing.

"Fuck, man," he said, but Ted just laughed, letting the bucket roll around as he pulled off his mask.

Virge lit a cigarette and jabbed his finger. "There's a reason we wear those you know."

"What is it?" Ted asked.

"What?"

"The reason."

Virge turned back to his writing, brain stumbling through a haze. Ted kicked the bucket around the floor.

"How many legs do goats have?" Virge asked.

🖫

"I never told her," Ted said.

"That you loved her?"

"Yeah."

Ted was sitting on the yoga ball. It was expelling air, but slowly, so right now it looked like a beanbag chair. Or a large potato.

Virge blew out more smoke, tired of hearing the same old stories. "Maybe you should have," he offered.

"Would have ruined the mood."

Virge thought he saw a ship out in the distance, but didn't say anything. It wasn't for them, too large, and he didn't want to excite Ted. He had to live with the man.

"I paid her, of course," Ted said. "Even tipped her. A lot. Forty bucks. Sometimes eighty. I gave her a pair of glasses once. Didn't even hire her that night. Nice ones, sunglasses. You know, like they have in... the movie... place." He paused, fingers twitching, then shook his head, giving up. "So do you think that counted?"

"Counted as what?" Virge asked.

"As telling her I loved her."

Virge shrugged.

🖫

Ted was bouncing a ball against the wall. Virge asked where he got it.

"From the cabinet."

The ball made a thud against the metal wall. Thud. Thud. Thud.

"What time," thud "is it?" Thud, Ted asked.

"Don't know." Thud.

"I wish" thud "they gave us" thud "a clock." Thud.

Thud. Thud. Thud.

"Who?"

💾

The boy was thin now, standing on top of that hill.

"We talked about taking a cruise," Ted said, the ball flying up, cresting just below the fan, and falling back in his hand.

The goat chewed on some of the grass. There was still some grass there. The boy just swayed, shouting something weakly.

"Well I talked about it mostly. But she listened."

There was a man by the fence at the bottom of the hill. Sometimes that man watched, and wondered what the boy was saying.

"We could see the world, I told her."

If he could hear the boy, maybe that would make the difference. He wasn't heartless.

Ted missed and dropped the ball, where it thudded over to Virge's chair. "It's funny," he said. "But she had seen more of the world than me, really, if you think about it. In her own way."

The words never came to him, so Virge shut the book and silently studied its featureless cover.

"Really though," Ted said, "she would have liked it. I know she would've."

💾

A boat came by on the mist. It was longer than most, very white, with thin stripes on its edge. Its windows were black, and Virge couldn't see anyone in them. He wondered, again, if they could see him.

"SSZSZSZZSSSZZS" said the intercom.

"I know," Virge said, "he's coming out."

Ted finished affixing the mask to his face, and closed the door, knocking back a few snakes of mist that had wandered into their booth. He clunked down the dock.

"SZSZZZSSZSZZSZZZZS"

"He's going to set it, calm down."

Virge flicked on the switch at the back of the TV, and watched through the tripod of cameras outside as Ted started to turn the crank at the back end of the dock.

"ZSSZSZS"

Virge scribbled down an idea for his book, and then pressed the intercom again.

"Cargo?"

"ZSSSSSSZSSZZSSZSZSZSSZSZS ZSZSZZSZSZS"

"That's double."

"SZSZSZSZSZZ"

"Typhoon? I guess that'll do it. What's your code?"

"SSZZZSZSZSZSZSZSZ"

"I don't know."

"SZSZSZSZSZS"

"Yeah try that."

"SSSSSSZZZZZSSSSSZZZZ"

"Hmm... Checks out."

The whole booth shook as the crank slammed against its end. Ted gave it another push to check, and nodded to himself.

"ZSSZSZSSSSZZSZSSZSZSSZ"

"Yep, you're clear."

"SZZ"

"Yeah, you too."

The boat floated through as Ted clunked back. Virge watched it sink below, into the mist that swirled in like claws above its deck, pulling it down, beyond the border.

💾

Virge puffed out his smoke toward the table and twirled the ball in the cloud. It formed little smoke hurricanes for a second or two.

"You ever been in love?" Ted asked.

Virge spun the ball again, a bit too hard and it slipped off the table, bouncing out its thuds.

"Depends on your definition, I guess," Virge said, turning to pick up his notebook.

"Like someone you could escape with, you know?" Ted pulled himself over a few feet in pursuit of his ball, before giving up.

"Escape what?" Virge said.

"Would it kill you to just give me straight answer every once in a while?"

Virge clicked his pen. "Maybe."

💾

"I don't think I'm supposed to be here," Ted said. His legs hung off his chair.

Virge was playing with the gas mask, turning it around in his hand, poking each cheek and lenspiece. It was standard issue, aside from the fact that it had no filter.

AT THE BORDER POST

"Who is?" Virge asked finally.

"I'm serious," Ted said. "I'm not even sure where we are."

Virge gave a laugh, turning the mask over in his hand. He wondered if he had removed the filter at some point, or if there just never was one.

"I don't even remember applying for this job." Ted stared, unfocused, at the floor beneath him.

"Take a walk," Virge said, tossing him the mask. "You just need to clear your mind a bit."

🖫

Virge wrote a mountain into his story.

"It was a Tuesday, the last time I saw her," Ted said, eyes cloudy.

Virge just grunted and continued to write.

"Yeah. We were at the parking lot of a 7-11. I was going to pick her up. I drove down, and parked. She was there, but she wasn't alone."

There were trees on the mountain. Big and green, full of fruit. Virge missed trees.

"Alan was there," Ted said. "He was a big guy, shoulders like a gorilla's... shoulders. Big is what I mean."

"Sure." The boy tried to eat the grass, like the goat, but spat it out.

"He was there and he was upset. Real upset. He had found my letters, I think. No, that's wrong, he told me that *she* found the letters. I don't think she was upset. She didn't seem upset."

It was impossible to write and listen. Virge would rather write, but he had to live with Ted, so he closed the book.

"Yeah, so, he said I should mind my own business." Ted shook his head. "I mean, he took her away first, right? It wasn't her home, so what was the difference?"

Virge had heard this all before, and the story never seemed to change. But he shrugged anyway, for Ted's sake.

"I didn't even say I would do it," he continued, "just that I wanted to. Take her traveling, anywhere she wanted. A cruise and everything, you know?" Ted stared out the window.

"There's something there!" he shouted, jumping up and pointing.

Virge followed his hand.

"I don't see anything," he said.

"No, no it's big!"

There was just dark blue above darker blue.

"Hey! Hey!" Ted waved his hands over his head. "Over here!"

💾

"Anyway, Alan wasn't happy," Ted said, sitting down finally. "He told me I shouldn't come around again. Shouldn't talk to her. Said it didn't matter how much I spent. She showed him the sunglasses, and he got even madder. Made it real, I think."

"He said if I ever came around again he'd make me sorry. That's what he said. Make me sorry. I already said I was sorry."

"He said people like me made it hard to run a business."

"He said she didn't love me."

"I punched him. He got in my face and I punched him. I don't know what he would have done if I hadn't, but I punched him."

"He went D-O-W-N. Down. Crack." Ted smacked his hands. "Like that. Loudest noise I ever heard. Like a pumpkin hitting the ground from a thousand miles up."

"What happened after that?" Virge asked.

"After?"

💾

The mist rolled off the railings outside. Virge smoked and wrote. Ted noticed the TV.

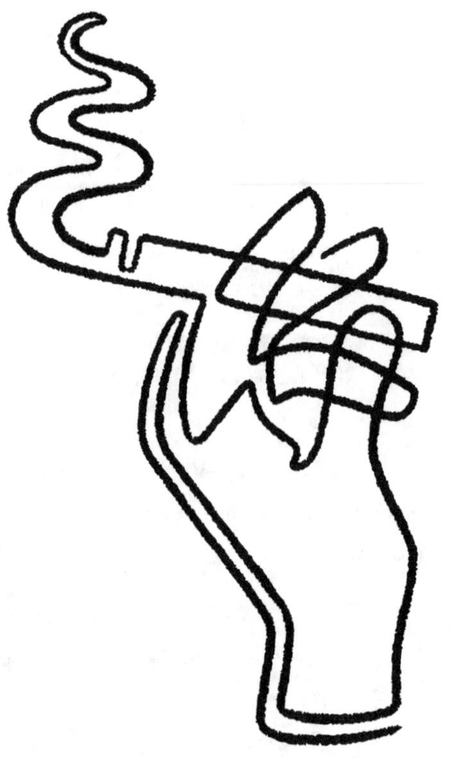

"Oh nice!" he said. "When they bring that in?"

Click. Bzzzz. Click. Bzzzz. Click. Bzzzz.

"Figures," Ted said, "not a thing on it."

Virge opened up the cabinet and slipped the ball in.

💾

Ted was sleeping. Or maybe he just thought he was sleeping, sitting back on his chair, breathing slowly, eyes closed, like he remembered. The sky hinted at yellow, but Virge knew it was only taunting him. Sure enough, it soon turned blue.

The mist rolled over the dock, leaving little eddies that drained through puncture holes.

Virge chewed on the burnt butt of his cigarette as he put down the last word on the last line of the book. The boy had starved again. He and the goat spent the last five pages walking up, then down, then up, then down the hill. Looking for something, but never near the fence, never near the man. Finally the boy collapsed, face down at the end corner of the final page.

Virge shut it, and snuck past Ted. Ted didn't wake up, or if he wasn't asleep, he didn't move. Virge took the key out of his pocket and opened the door to the basement. Foot after foot, he climbed down the ladder into the dark.

Every step clanging

As he descended

Down.

Down.

Down.

Down.

Virge reached the bottom, and landed his foot on a hill of red rectangles. Embedded in the wall beside the ladder was a shelf. It held a single empty book, as always. He took the blank notebook and shuffled through its pages, expecting the nothing that he saw, feeling the familiar, expected, disappointment. He shrugged and tossed his completed notebook into the shadows.

It bounced down the hill, deep into the dark, smashing off jutting ridges, clearing leather-bound crevasses, and sliding down scarps of open pages. It careened past its uncountable brothers, past pages of boys who starved and goats who ate and the man by the fence who did nothing.

He waited to listen to moan of the sea above, and felt the whipping wind of an empty horizon. The air was cold down here, but at least there was no mist.

After some time he couldn't measure, he put the fresh notebook in his pocket and turned back, lifting his left foot onto the ladder rung, then bringing up his other. In this way he clanged his way up and up and up and up:

Each clang summoning a far distant echo.

HAILEY PIPER

REPTILE

181 Downing Lane had to be the ugliest apartment building Lorna Camille had ever seen. The broken glass, barred windows, and buckling northern wall of poorly-set bricks said it had rejected all attempts at human habitation, as if every person who stepped inside was swallowed up, good intentions and all.

Why Serene wanted to meet here, Lorna couldn't imagine. This looked a better site for a murder than a miracle, and they had been so at odds of late that Lorna could believe Serene might kill her here. It was unbecoming of sisters to fight over a man, Lorna thought, but fortunately there was no real fight. Serene didn't know how far off track she was about Ben Westler's feelings. He was going to propose, become Serene's brother-in-law. It would be unbecoming of one sister to murder another, of course.

But Serene had promised a miracle, and when she appeared around the curb, she looked in a better mood than Lorna had seen all year. Her smile radiated down her white jacket and pants. "Inside."

Lorna followed through the rusty iron door, into a lobby of patchy carpeting, soiled by rats, up untrust-worthy steel steps, past peeling walls, shedding their wallpaper. There was no graffiti. Mid-city, rundown building, no evidence of kids with spray paint, no leavings by the homeless. It was unheard of, but not quite a miracle.

"How far?"

"Third floor, here we are." Serene left the steps and led Lorna down a hall of broken doors, their destroyed apartments bare and rotting. All but one. "This is it. The miracle."

"It's a door," Lorna said.

Serene stared at her the way a teacher might when a student just isn't trying. "Open it."

"Serene, if there are cockroaches-" Lorna grasped the filthy knob with her shirt sleeve and pressed against the steel door.

Humid air breathed across their faces the moment the door cracked open, a seal being broken. Then came the sunlight. Not the gray, smoggy pretender to sunlight that Downing Lane might see, but harsh, unbroken rays of the sun. Lorna had to shield her eyes until they adjusted. Dry dirt spread from the door's other side, up to greening fields and lonesome trees that shot up taller than the apartment building. A shadow walked the distant horizon, its neck stretched to the sky.

Lorna's fingers gripped the doorframe, her wrist in the cold hall, her fingers in the warm sunshine. "What am I seeing?"

"A long, long time ago." Serene brushed past, poked her head through the doorway. "Have you ever smelled air so clean?"

The smells were foreign to Lorna. She had hardly ever left New York, let alone visited the baked, otherworldly plains ahead. "It's prehistoric. How did this happen?"

"I don't know. But I knew you'd love it."

Lorna hid a smile. Of course she would. The whole world would, wouldn't they? "And you only showed me."

"I wouldn't want to pollute the past with every gawker in the city. Now, here's the incredible part." Serene said it like this wasn't the discovery of a lifetime. She clawed the soil for a pebble and tossed it into the air. Then she drew back and pulled the door shut.

"What was that about?"

"Would you say it's landed by now?"

"Of course."

Serene pressed the door again, the same crack in the air. The pebble hit the earth. A small blue lizard shot from around the outside of the door, chomped the pebble, realized it wasn't food, and skittered off.

"The other side only moves when the door's open," Lorna said.

"You could observe something, leave, come back, have it still be there. A lot more interesting than teaching history, isn't it?" Serene slipped inside and waved a hand. "Come on. We'll get a tan while we're here."

Lorna followed onto the crisp earth. Behind her, the door opened from the foot of a cliff, its stone face broken by the rectangular doorway. Chilly air wafted out from the apartment hall. The sun was burdensome, the air heavy, but those were small inconveniences. Serene was right. She had found a miracle.

"How did you find it?"

Serene neared a tree that was millions of years old. Or perhaps it was only five. "Would you believe I was looking for a quiet place to kill you?" She waited for Lorna to make a face and then gave a shrill laugh. "You're so silly."

"Yes. *I'm* silly. Me." Lorna stared at the distant shadow. It walked on four legs, its tail and neck reaching long as a city block, best she could tell. If she listened, she could hear its footsteps slam the ground. They weren't reptiles, but with that echo, it was small wonder they had

been called thunder lizards.

At her feet, the blue lizard circled, curious. Why wouldn't it be? It had never seen a human before, would probably go extinct before mankind could start hunting it.

There were bigger, less benign creatures in this period of time, Lorna remembered. The kind that would've happily hunted humans had they survived to see them exist. She scanned the trees, the plains, saw nothing she might view as a threat.

Except Serene was gone.

"We should stick together!" Lorna shouted, and then brought her fist to her lips. Shouting could summon the wrong attention. Showing the miracle had been sweet, but visiting was a mistake. They didn't belong here. "Serene, where are you?"

Lorna jogged to the tree where she'd last seen her sister, circled it, but there was no one. Footsteps in the soil led back toward the cliff, the door. Her eyes followed.

Serene stood in the doorway. Her white jacket and pants were gone, replaced by a black dress that seemed out of season for the chill in New York. Had she brought other clothes? "Evening, Lorie. Just seeing how you're getting on."

"How I'm what?" Lorna started

toward Serene.

The door was closing.

"Wait a minute, Ser—"

Her ears didn't register the door slamming shut.

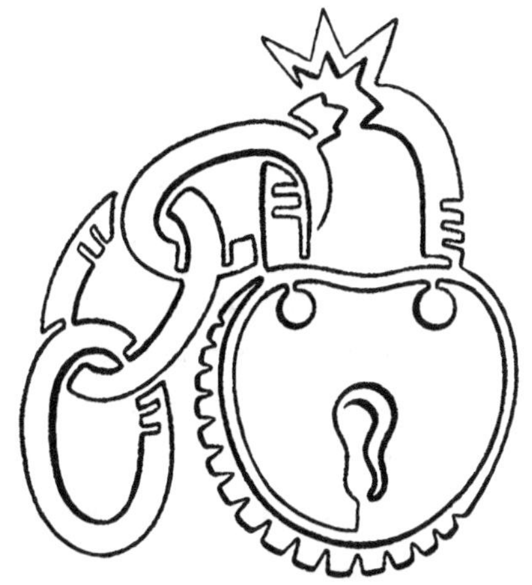

Aden couldn't stop fidgeting while Bry cut the steel open. Not that he thought they would get caught—no one came to Downing anymore—but 181, like its sibling buildings, was a deathtrap. Rickety stairs, crumbling walls. No one cared about this place. Which made it all the less likely for anything valuable to be stashed here.

But Bry was insistent. Despite the crumbling of the neighborhood, the city, the country, the world, this door had remained firm. Rusty, but firm, as if held in place by what waited behind it, maybe vacuum-sealed. The snapped padlock clattered on the grimy floor in pieces. Bry set down his bolt cutters and rubbed his hands together. He and Aden pressed the door open together.

"—ene!"

Lorna burst through the doorway, slamming into the two boys. They collapsed in a pile on filthy debris.

"Serene?" Lorna scrambled off, onto her feet, up against the wall. "Serene, where are you?" Her voice rang empty through the hall. She looked to the two kids she'd plowed into. They looked not half as rundown as the building, but they certainly weren't doing well. One of them had eyes on her purse. "Did you see another woman here? About my height, my—she looked a lot like me."

Humming static erupted from the boys' mouths. "NameAden."

"NameBry. IDmade. Whysnailspeakadult. Wego?"

Lorna watched their mouths. They made odd shapes with their lips and jaws, as if unused to speaking. "You're going too fast."

"Noneuralsnailspeakslowgoes." Bry shrugged.

"Can you tell me what's happening to me?"

Aden knelt, picked up the padlock fragments, and placed them in Lorna's hands. Then he pointed at the door.

Her hands began to quiver. It wasn't possible. Serene couldn't. She would've found a way to make money off this miracle. What the padlock suggested, what it meant, was unthinkable. Lorna's fists curled around the fragments and threw them down the rickety stairs. They clanged a few times and disappeared.

"Okay." Lorna grasped her head. "Okay, okay. Okay." The implications were setting in. She wasn't a stupid person. Now her mouth worked at odd angles, struggling to form the question. "One last thing. Can you tell me what year it is?"

They told her. She shoved them aside and ran.

Downing Lane was hotter than when she left, hotter than she could ever remember the city. The sky looked pale, like its blue had been put through the washer too many times. She recognized the neighborhood's bones, but not its flesh. It had been left to wear out, go rotten, 181 being only the start.

She wanted to go home, but no cabs were driving through here. The subway, by sheer laziness of the powers that be, had not changed much, the pits still spewing their baked garbage smells that somehow lured most of the city down below. Subway cars had been remodeled, a couple of routes adjusted, but the map was recognizable.

The turnstiles were not. There were no sliders for plastic or paper tickets, no slots for tokens, no machines to change money into passage. Each passenger slid their arm along the side. The turnstile either let them push through or gave a buzzing alarm.

One young man tried to jump the turnstile and metro police were on him like flies. "NameTrad, IDmade," he said, his words as involuntary as a sneeze.

Lorna didn't dare try it. She returned to the surface.

Walking was misery in this heat. She carried her jacket block after block, into less rundown parts of the city. Floating lights bustled above, their advertisements adrift from window to window. Everything seemed so quiet, like the world she had left inside the door. If people were talking, she couldn't hear them. There was only the trample of footsteps and the gentle rush of silent cars. They seemed to clank together and break apart at each street, but her head was too dizzy to piece out how it all worked.

In time, she found a library. By some luck, no one needed to swipe their arms to get inside. There were even people talking within, most of them elderly and sequestered to their own section. Anyone could pick up an electronic slate from the front and walk it wherever they pleased, select what they wanted to know. Not too different from any smartphone. Lorna hadn't bothered to look at hers. After her meeting with Aden and Bry, she knew. This was as much a place for reading as for gathering, the way libraries had been in Lorna's time.

There was only one person to search for. Serene Camille. And when that didn't work, she tried Serene Westler. They were married three years after Ben was supposed to propose to Lorna. They had two children, both deceased now, and two grandchildren, also deceased. Ben, likewise, was deceased, his obituary and that of his children and his children's children all matters of public record, easy to find.

Lorna pressed the slate away and covered her face. She had only left Ben a few hours ago to meet Serene at Downing Lane. Hours and years. She slammed her fists on the table, but the collision couldn't bring back the time. In a way, Serene really had brought her to that building to murder her. Murder her time, her place. Murder and robbery. The more she thought about it, the harder she sobbed.

People were staring, she felt their eyes. What a different kind of city this had become.

If only Serene really understood what she had done, the impact. Finding her seemed impossible, but she wasn't dead or else her obituary would have been available, like the others. She was somewhere out in the world. Lorna didn't think the hunt was possible. This world wasn't hers.

She asked the librarian if there was a way for her to make a phone call. Translating what she meant by that took some doing, but eventually the librarian pulled out a paper-thin slip of plastic and helped her call the Division of Public Protection, some national form of law enforcement that Lorna saw no point in coming to understand. She was still in this world for one purpose. Whosoever could reunite the sisters Camille, she would go to them.

"You won't believe what I'm about to tell you," she said to the phone.

DPP officers arrived to detain her. She was clearly unhinged to be telling stories like that. What they couldn't figure out was who she was. Their machines couldn't scan her arms or head. She was processed through paperwork, seen by a physician, and then by a psychologist. Through it all, what she said and how she said it triggered alarms in their heads.

She endured two weeks of testing and procedures. Every step of the way, she was compliant, taking every measure within her power to convince the authorities that she was a gift, not a threat. That became harder the more they believed her story. When they finally let her show them the door at 181 Downing, they brought her to different experts. They had her sign all kinds of documents, blind to how worthless those were in the scope of what she was telling them. She agreed to everything they wanted. There was little left to lose.

After four weeks, she met the Joint Chiefs of Staff. After another, she met in private with the President, little more than a figurehead, now. He comprehended little of what she meant, but assured her it was an honor to meet her.

A month and a half after she turned herself in to authorities, they brought her to the hospital in the dead of night. Armed guards in tactical gear secured the stairwell, elevators, and the seventh floor east wing, a senior hospice section. There, Lorna walked into a private room and closed the door.

An elderly woman, unrecognizable in her layers of wrinkled, folded skin, lay in a hospital bed. She would never leave this bed, rooted by plastic tubes that ensured fluid came and went at an even pace. Her eyes opened at the sound of the door and widened when they noticed Lorna's approach.

"Oh." Her jaw slackened, moaning, and she tried to skirt back in the bed, but her bony limbs were too frail to slide her deflated body anywhere. "Lorie, you've come for me. I'm sorry. Christ, my eyes. I can't see you. I can't see your death."

That Serene mistook her for a ghost made Lorna smile. "I'm right here." Her hand stroked the blanket until it found Serene's fingers and squeezed. "Almost exactly the way you left me."

Serene's free hand reached across her, to Lorna's middle, and brushed her fingertips against an abdomen of real flesh and bone. "You're real. You got out."

"I was let out." Lorna squeezed harder, leaned close to Serene's face. "Why wasn't it you who let me out?"

"I forgot where the door was."

"You put a padlock on it."

A wretched smile wormed its way through the folds of Serene's cheeks. "I lost the key, too."

Lorna sat on the bed. Her free hand reached Serene's tired face, stroked her leathery skin, her wispy, shedding hair. "You could've changed the world when you found that door. History would've idolized you. Instead, all that door looked like was a cruel way to get rid of me. Why didn't you just kill me?"

"Wouldn't have gotten away with it." Serene hacked out what might have been a laugh. "I didn't plan it like this. We went inside and I thought we might

REPTILE

let bygones be bygones. But you were so infatuated. You made it so easy to close the door and leave you."

"How many months did it take?"

"With Ben? Less time than you think." Another hacking, awful laugh.

"You took him. You took my life."

Lorna's hand found Serene's neck. Hard to believe there was a throat buried deep in all that skin. She thought she might say something snappy, a great telling off before she crushed her sister's windpipe, watched her squirm and struggle, her weak hands grasping in futility for just a little bit more life.

There was no point. She didn't need to hurt Serene any worse. Serene only had to stop living. And she did, once all the death throes played out exactly as Lorna had envisioned them.

When the machines said Serene was dead, her tubes ceased their function and the door opened. Normal times, that would be a nurse or doctor or both, come to resuscitate or announce the time of death. Instead there was only an officer in tactical gear. Lorna had collected her end of the arrangement. Time to pay up.

🖫

"We have significant gaps in our history," a bald man in a pleasant suit explained as he sat Lorna down in a room full of machines like she had never seen. His "snailspeak" was refreshing. "The early twenty-first century is almost a lost era to us. We don't even have reference to most of its culture and numerous historical facts have been skewed."

"You want me to patch the holes."

"I want you to write everything you can think of. EverInk is far better at lasting than what people worked with digitally in your time, and it's ecologically sound. It should last. We will give you a copy of what you've made, along with what we have. We can fit it on a bead no bigger than a drop of water."

Lorna told him she would need a bigger physical container than that, but she did what he wanted. Her writing referenced anything she could think of— politics, discussions, movies, music. She wrote until she couldn't think of anything left to write. Most of it was only allusions to events and media. With no way to reclaim what was lost, at least there was a record that they had existed.

Her next task was harder. She wrote the differences she could understand between her time and this new one, decades later. The government would provide an archive of all their known data, but her observations were scientifically unique and therefore of unprecedented value.

"A genuine time traveler," the man said. She never learned his name.

The more she learned about this time, the less interest she had. She tried not to let disgust pollute her writing, but some disdain was inevitable. This was a bleak world she didn't belong in. The authorities seemed to know it as well as she did. It made it easy to agree with their plans.

She didn't even attend Serene's service. If there were people who might miss her, Lorna didn't want to know.

When every recording was made and Lorna had rested, the man and other officials escorted her back to 181 Downing Lane. No surprise, it had been cordoned off, made a black site. Even satellites couldn't touch it. Government scientists had spent the past few weeks poking and prodding, but if any of them understood the doorway and its mechanism they never explained it to her.

The man in the suit shook her hand and introduced another man. "This is Diop. He'll be our ambassador to the future. Hopefully a brighter one."

Diop shook her hand as well. "I look forward to getting to know each other."

Lorna scowled at the nameless man. "You didn't explain how it works?"

"They explained. I understand." Diop smiled like someone good at pretending. "It's difficult to process, though."

"Try not having a choice." Lorna opened the door. Prehistoric warmth breathed down her face, not so different from the warmth of the future city. She wondered how hot it would be when she next emerged.

Diop had signed a waiver that he could not sue the government of the future for the years he would miss. He seemed to think he was headed for a better future. Maybe he was right.

There were no supplies to drop off. This was probably the least expensive mission the government had ever embarked on, and yet with all the overhead and oversight, Lorna imagined every step she took would cost millions. Funny, she hadn't thought about money since she emerged. It had seemed to consume so many of her thoughts before Serene found the door.

"Do you have a family?" Lorna asked.

"Siblings," Diop said. "No wife or kids, if that's what you mean."

"Good."

The nameless man seemed befuddled at last. He was talking to scientists, military personnel, but between every empty handshake, he glanced Lorna's way. "You've done so much for us. Are you sure there isn't anything else you need? One hospital visit hardly seems fair."

Was he being coy? Did he not know they let Lorna get away with murder? They told her that was okay, if only she did them a favor. She wondered how many such favors were parsed out every day, and then remembered none of that mattered, because almost everyone present would be dead the next time this door opened.

She had only one more request. "Don't let anyone forget me this time."

💾

A rumble ran through the forest of fungal trees, shaking their trunks so hard that a cloud of yellow-white spores rained across the trampled path. Most days, this was a still place. The people had tried to cut it down, make the pathway easier, but it was used so seldom that they could not remember to cut, and often nature fought back. A lizard the size of six people lay across the path, dormant as the forest, and the people stepped off the path to bypass it. Too many had been eaten by lizards last time. That, they remembered.

At last, the procession reached the great stone cavern secured by the Ancestors who first found the Door to Eternity. None of the carnivores could enter here; they were too large. Only small creatures and the people could slip through the dark doorway, guided by firelight, to where the cold slab of rusted metal stood embedded inside ancient stone.

They squatted down in a cluster, their head caps touching, and were silent.

Elder Lavia pressed their bulbous arms together, overgrown with spore infections, and led the people in prayer. Soon those infections would burst, the coming of new children, but before that, Lavia would see the door open again. So few of the people survived to witness two Openings. Lavia had remained celibate until now. Few could last for so long.

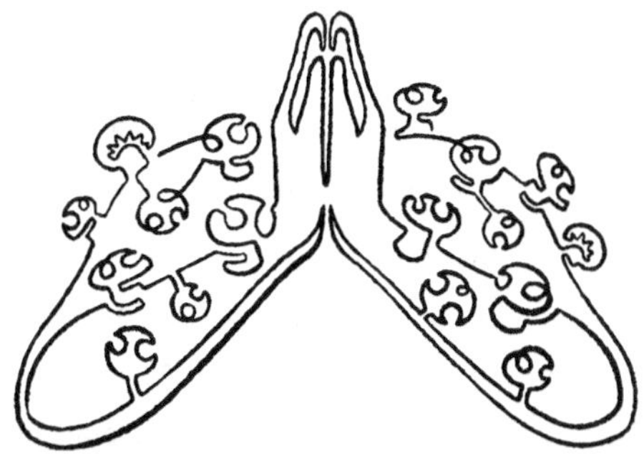

When prayers were finished, Lavia shuffled to the door and slid their arm inside a twining hoop of weeds. There was another way to open the door, a small, metal shape that stuck out midway along one side, but none of the people could grasp it, and whatever let the door swing had been long ago replaced. The Ancestors, in their wisdom, made the opening easier. All children of the people had a right to the knowledge within. The miracle within.

The Door to Eternity swung open. A cool breeze floated across Lavia, same as when they were young. Sometimes that breeze seemed imagined, as if no air could feel so refreshing, but here it came, good as Lavia remembered it. They could have stood there for a day, but today was not about them.

It was about her.

The last human emerged into the stone cavern. Many of the people began to hum in disquiet. They had never seen her like before, not even in historical art. Lavia was embarrassed, but remembered that shortsightedness was why the Door to Eternity was opened every hundred years. So that Lorna Camille could gift the people with the truth.

She widened her maw and bared her teeth, but Lavia wasn't afraid like the children in the crowd. Lorna did this last time, and Lavia knew she wasn't going to eat the people.

"You look familiar. Was Lavia your sire? Your grandsire?" She spoke the people's language of hums and grunts, but with a strange accent.

Lavia's sire had wondered if that was how the people spoke a hundred years before, but Lavia knew better. Lorna was doing her best. "I am Lavia myself."

"Then it's good to see you again. I just left you."

"Short, for you. For me, a lifetime."

Lavia spoke to the people in a faster speech, the flashing colors that writhed across their cap. Sometimes the colors were hard to discern beneath their many growths, the coming of many children. They told the people that Lorna was here to clarify the people's history, to explain what had been, and to record what was new.

The cavern had been prepared for her. She needed water, like the people, but ate things like the carnivores, the spawn sacks that weeds made, even parts of the trees. She made waste like the carnivores, but Lavia knew this was hard for her now. It was why they wanted so badly to remain celibate, wait until the door reopened.

When Lorna sat on the soft bed of weeds that was built for her, Lavia squatted beside her and showed off their arms. "Do you see? I am with children. Like you."

Lorna stroked her abdomen, where long ago a woman whose name the people would never know had prodded to be sure Lorna was real. She didn't touch Lavia's arms, but looked closely at them. "They will be beautiful children. I'm sorry they won't meet you like I was lucky enough to."

Lavia hoped that would be recorded. Maybe Lorna would meet their children or children's children at the next Opening and tell them the greatness of their sire and grandsire.

Seeing Lavia sit beside the last human encouraged the people. They shuffled closer to Lorna, first the historians who wanted her to settle disagreements, and then the most curious, the young. They waited at her feet while history changed before them.

Lorna held a slab of dried tree in her hands and pointed one slender digit. "You let your geography data skew. This is how the continents were shaped."

She retrieved a black hunk of char to draw corrections. Small beads dotted her flesh. It was written that those beads contained everything the humans ever learned, long dead before the time of the people, but Lorna said there were no machines left that could read them. It was fortunate she was able to learn the language of the people as it evolved.

When the historians finished, half the day had passed and many of the children had wandered off to play. Lavia was embarrassed again that they would squander this opportunity. Most, if not all of them, would be dead by the next century when the door opened once more.

One small child nestled close to Lorna's side. "Were you alone?"

"I'm never alone," Lorna said, and stroked her middle again.

"But someone to talk to."

"Sometimes other humans would come with me. They would stay a couple rounds, but after that, it gets hard. A little ways into the future is interesting. Too much is culture shock. A lot, and you don't feel like you'll ever belong. Once, a lot of humans went inside with me, for refuge. The door only opened for us because of a rock slide. When they found out the other humans were gone, they went off together to repopulate the world. They didn't make it. Eventually none of us do."

The child pointed at Lorna's middle. "Did one of them put the baby in you?"

"Oh, this one's father died before I went inside." Lorna stared past the child, toward the back of the cavern. The door awaited her, as it always had. "He died long ago."

Lorna bore no colors atop her head to reveal her feelings, but the tired slump in her body language told Lavia a truth unwritten in the people's histories. The last human bore the knowledge of the people, of the humans, of the world, but she had a story of her own that she told no one. And had Lavia asked, she would have widened her maw, friendly, told them it was nothing worth telling. Maybe that was true. Lavia still wished to know. Lorna might have thought it inconsequential, but she was the only living human, and it was the only living human's story. In countless years, perhaps even she would be gone.

That would be so far ahead that Lavia couldn't fathom it.

The day drew on, Lorna passing out information, the children failing to understand it, but their minds awakened with possibility. As last time, the people argued whether one or more of them should accompany Lorna, to be thrust ahead into the hopeful progress of a century to come. While most thought it was a good idea, none wanted to volunteer. The people were making strides with vine-work, teaching it to peel away layers of earth, uncover what remained of geological layers that might be useful someday. They wanted to see that progress unfold.

Lorna slept awhile, at which time half the people left. By night there was only Lavia and a handful of historians, all of whom would leave before morning when the lizards became most active. When Lorna awoke, it was time.

"I loved seeing you again, Lavia," she said. "I hope your grandchildren will meet me at the door next."

Lavia would will it so. "Is there nothing we can do for you?"

Lorna stepped through the door, into the coolness of many millions of years ago. "Would you leave the door open for a few moments? I've spent eons here, but I've hardly taken the time to know this place. Not since the start."

Lavia understood there were more dangerous creatures than the lizards on the far side of the door, carnivores that could consume even the last human, but there was no refusing Lorna. They let the door hang open and waited, watching her.

She sat on a dry patch of soil, legs crossed beneath her, the weight of her middle nestled like an egg on her lap. Black shapes crossed the distant sky. Somewhere distant, a tree crashed, thoughtlessly trampled at the edge of a forest where a nameless animal that weighed many tons had let its tail swing wild. Creatures were dying, others hatching. A small, blue lizard slid past Lorna's feet, the same that had mistaken a rock for food, minutes and eons ago. Scales had frayed along its neck where it was beginning to shed a skin.

They were alike, she and the lizard, both timeless here, and yet shedding their layers. The world beyond the door was her skin. Each time the door opened, the last time became near useless, only evidence that there had been a before and a promise that there would be more skins to shed. Everything that mattered in one instant became a relic in the next. Arguments, money, thoughts, children. All of it, dead scales peeling off a lizard's hide.

Her hands clasped her swollen gut, palms pressed. Beneath them, a kick.

She wondered how many more centuries she would visit before the labor pains began and she was forced to give birth in a world that could neither understand nor help her and her baby. Maybe they both would die. Maybe there was something wrong with the baby, afflicted by the past, the future, the door.

Or maybe, someday, there would be a new last human.

She had dragged this out enough, could feel Lavia's nervousness. The people had lives to return to, and she did not. She glanced over her shoulder and gave them a final smile. "That's fine. I know you're anxious. You may close the door now."

COVER ART: ERIKA SCHNATZ

Erika Schnatz is a doodler and designer who lives in Portland, Oregon, with her husband and the cutest (and least well-behaved) dog in the world. By day, she works at Image Comics as a production artist. In her free time she creates comics and illustrations. Every March, she runs a tournament of cuteness called Cute K.O.: 16 characters go head-to-head until a champion is crowned at the end of the month. It's fun. The Cute K.O. universe expands each year as new characters are added to the competition.

Erika's work is created with a mix of traditional and digital tools; she tends to do most drawing and linework with pencils and pens before scanning a piece to be colored in Photoshop. Recently, she has experimented with Risograph printing and paint markers. She likes making things that are colorful, humorous, and a little weird.

Erika's work can be found at erikaschnatz.com and @erikaschnatz on Instagram and Twitter.

PLANET SCUMM: What current or recent projects are you excited about?

ERIKA SCHNATZ: I've started collecting a list of "Dream Dog" suggestions from people I know, and I'm planning on doodling some of the suggestions throughout August (and maybe longer than that if I feel especially motivated). They are wonderful to imagine, like a pocket-sized dog or a bioluminescent dog (great to take on camping trips!). I also plan on drawing a Dogbus, for people who think the Catbus from *My Neighbor Totoro* could be improved if the animal was switched out. ;)

PS: In one sentence, describe your favorite artist without using their name.

ES: Multi-talented Disney concept artist who had an incredible eye for color and was a goddess with gouache.

PS: If you could design the movie poster for any movie, what would it be?

ES: I am huge fan of anything The Lonely Island puts out, (*Popstar* is criminally underrated and everyone should go watch it) so my dream would be to work with The Lonely Island gentlemen on a movie poster for a live action/animation hybrid film. Maybe based on my Cute K.O. character, Grandpa Breadstick

(*Pictured below*). My husband and I have built up a detailed and very bizarre backstory for Grandpa Breadstick, so it would be amazing to bring that character to life on screen with the help of my favorite comedy rap trio. Maybe it would be a photo-realistic depiction of Grandpa Breadstick with almost no explanatory text. It would be like nothing you've ever seen before, most definitely.

PS: In the inevitable war between robots and humans, what side will you take and why?

ES: I'm siding with the robots. Humans have done a great job of causing irrevocable damage to the environment, so I think it's time for someone (or something else) to take over and right this ship. And hey, in a robot-led society, I bet public transit would always run on time.

SPOT ILLUSTRATIONS: ALYSSA ALARCÓN SANTO

Alyssa Alarcón Santo is a full-time illustrator based out of Portland, OR, where she lives with her writer husband. Her love of meticulous hand lettering, cynical philosophy, and all things literary are common threads in her artwork. To pay the bills, she can be found creating commercial illustration work for clients like National Novel Writing Month and Xbox. She also writes an ongoing series of memoir comics, Traitor Legs, about her journey through newfound disability.

While Alyssa most frequently works digitally with a combination of a Wacom Cintiq and an iPad Pro, she also dabbles with traditional media—usually Copic markers, Posca paint pens, or acrylic ink and dip pens. She loves to draw subjects that are detailed, structural, and, dare I say it, even a little tedious. (We all need our Jerry Gergich.)

Her work can be found at alyssasantodesign.com or on Instagram at @alyssasantodesign.

PLANET SCUMM: What current or recent projects are you excited about?

ALYSSA SANTO: I've been working on a series of hand-lettered book stack paintings for the last year or so. The project has everything I love: copious amounts of research, meticulous serif lettering, and many, many reading lists. I've already done stacks for several fiction genres. This is pretty boring, but I'm pumped about some of the non-fiction stacks I have planned. I can't paint photorealistically, but I get so much joy from being able to closely recreate a physical object in my own style. I'm also working on a comic series with my husband. It's loosely based on my abuela (were she running her own minor crime empire).

PS: If you could design the movie poster for any movie, what would it be?

AS: My all-time favorite book is *House of Leaves* by Mark Danielewski. I know in my heart of hearts that an adaptation would be impossible to do correctly (and that anything they did make would just disappoint me). That being said, I would love to design a whole collection of posters for that elusive dream mini-series. It would be pretty difficult to capture the dread and the horror of the book, but I imagine it would be fun to borrow some optical illusion pointers from Escher.

PS: In one sentence, describe your favorite artist without using their name.

AS: Multi-disciplinary American artist from the early 1900s who is well-known for both architecture and glasswork.

PS: In the inevitable war between robots and humans, what side will you take and why?

AS: My legs are full of so much metal after all the surgeries I've had, I think I'm on the robot side by default. No joke though, I am constantly saying that my ultimate fantasy for life is to upload my mind into a robot body. I'd love to ditch this meat prison in which I live and move forward harder, better, faster, stronger.